Slow Down, MONKEY!

WRITTEN BY JESS FRENCH
ILLUSTRATED BY EEFJE KUIJL

EDITED BY JONNY LEIGHTON
DESIGNED BY JACK CLUCAS
COVER DESIGN BY JOHN BIGWOOD

J.F. – For Fenya, Ozra and little
monkeys everywhere; wishing you
peace amid our busy world,
full of expectations.

E.K. – For Guus & Fien.

First published in Great Britain in 2020 by Buster Books,
an imprint of Michael O'Mara Books Limited, 9 Lion Yard,
Tremadoc Road, London SW4 7NQ

W www.mombooks.com/buster f Buster Books 🐦 @BusterBooks

Text copyright © Jess French 2020

Illustrations copyright © Eefje Kuijl 2020

A CIP catalogue record for this book is available from the British Library.

ISBN: 978-1-78055-611-6

1 3 5 7 9 10 8 6 4 2

This book was printed in June 2020 by Leo Paper Products Ltd,
Heshan Astros Printing Limited, Xuantan Temple Industrial Zone,
Gulao Town, Heshan City, Guangdong Province, China.

Slow Down, MONKEY!

Buster Books

SWOOP! GRAB! WHOOSH! SWING!

Monkey's flying through the trees,
Tearing through the forest on her jungle vine trapeze.
She cries out, "It's my birthday!" for everyone to hear.
"I hope you're getting ready for the party of the year!"

She dashes past the dart frogs,
Who hop and croak,

"LOOK OUT!"

"So much to do," the monkey cries. "No time to hang about!
I need to find some music with a rocking jungle beat,
Some pretty decorations and a yummy cake to eat."

She bursts in on her feathered friends,

Who said they'd lend a hand,

And finds them in rehearsals for their funky forest band.

They strum on stems, they drum on trees,

Each songbird big and small ...

CRASH, BANG, SQUEAK, CRACK,

They don't sound good AT ALL!

She tries hard not to worry,
Zooming off to find the bear,
Who promised he would make a cake
for everyone to share.

"I've never baked before," he says,
"And something's not quite right.
There's **ICKY, STICKY, YUCKY, NASTY**
mud in every bite."

Monkey rushes through the vines
to make more preparations.
She really hopes that Tapir's had
more luck with decorations ...

"Oh Monkey, I'm so sorry,"
Says the tapir with a frown.
"I've tied my legs up in a knot
and landed upside down."

Monkey stops her forest rush,
She's feeling much too sad.
"It's all gone wrong," she thinks aloud.
"My party will be **BAD!**"

"I've tried to make it perfect,
I've tried to make it great.
I've rushed and bounced and dashed and zoomed,
But now it's far too late."

Then, somewhere up above her, comes a rustling in the trees.

She spots a creature moving like a gentle summer breeze.

"Hello, Sloth," says Monkey. "You're hanging very still.

I'm always rushing everywhere and all you do is chill."

Sloth looks up, he's very slow, no movement accidental.

His hair is long, his face is kind, his voice is soft and gentle.

"Come up here, take your time, wipe away that frown.

The key is to be patient, you just need to ... "

"SLOWWWW DOOOWWN!"

"Please don't rush and panic, worry, huff or sigh.
Your party will be perfect if you give these things a try.
LOOK around the forest and use your eyes to see
the rainbow-feathered parrots and the patterns on the trees."

"**BREATHE** in through your nostrils,
Take a great big sniff.
Smell the orchid's perfume and
the stink bug's nasty whiff.

Use your ears to **LISTEN**.
Hear the wind that blows.

FEEL the branches in your hands,
And earth beneath your toes."

Monkey takes the sloth's advice and slowly looks around.

The forest seems to pop and ping from canopy to ground.

"You see, my friend," the wise sloth says, "you didn't need to worry.

Now go and find the things you missed, when you were in a hurry."

Monkey helps untangle Tapir from the knotted vine.
"We don't need decorations, look, these flowers are divine."

Next, she finds the friendly bear,
Who cannot raise a smile.

"What will we eat?" he growls and grunts.
"The cake is oh so vile."

Monkey says, "Let's breathe in deep,
What can we find to munch?

These forest fruits smell nice and sweet,
A perfect birthday lunch!"

Now, Monkey just needs music,
That will get her party grooving.
She listens to the forest
and her body soon starts moving.

The treetop songbirds flap their wings
and burst out into song.
"It's party time," shouts Monkey,
"So come and dance along!"

Monkey and her friends arrive
(though Sloth is rather late).
They sing and dance and laugh and eat,
Her birthday party's great!

The mud feels squelchy round her toes,
It sploshes and it splatters.
At last, she sees, her friends are here,
And that's what really matters!

MONKEY AND HER FRIENDS

The animals in this story are based on real, endangered species that live in the hot and steamy rainforests of Colombia in South America. There's lots to learn about these amazing creatures.

WHITE-BELLIED SPIDER MONKEY
(Ateles belzebuth)

Spider monkeys love spending time with their friends and family, and they really love to play. They use their strong arms and tails to swing speedily through the branches of tall trees.

HARLEQUIN POISON DART FROGS
(Oophaga histrionica)

The brightly coloured skin of a harlequin poison dart frog is a warning. It means: "DON'T EAT ME, I'M DEADLY!" They start their lives as tadpoles living in water pooled in bromeliad plants.

RAINFOREST BIRDS

The rainforest is full of beautiful birds, including the toucan barbet, the Andean motmot, the Andean cock-of-the-rock, the paradise tanager and the quetzal, who all proudly show off their colourful feathers.

SPECTACLED BEAR
(Tremarctos ornatus)

Spectacled bears are gentle creatures, who are almost entirely vegetarian. Their favourite foods are bromeliad plants. (They'd better watch out for those poison dart frog tadpoles!)

SOUTH AMERICAN TAPIR
(Tapirus terrestris)

Tapirs are closely related to horses and rhinoceroses. When they are babies they are covered in stripes and dashes, which they lose as they grow.

BROWN-THROATED SLOTH
(Bradypus variegatus)

Brown-throated sloths live life in the slow lane. They spend most of their time hanging camouflaged in the trees, coming down just once a week when they need the toilet.

SLOTH SAYS, "SLOW DOWN!"

It can take a little practice to learn how to slow down and be more mindful of the world around you. So here are some tips to get you started:

LOOK — Sit quietly and look at your surroundings. How many different colours and lovely shapes can you see?

BREATHE — Take a deep, slow breath in through your nose. Hold it for a few seconds and slowly release it through your mouth.

LISTEN — Listen carefully to the world all around you. Try to identify five different sounds.

FEEL — Close your eyes and concentrate on what you can feel. Is the air hot or cold? Is the ground hard or soft?

If you're feeling rushed and stressed like Monkey, following these steps once a day could help you feel happier and more relaxed – just like Sloth!